"Clara of Crooked Creek"

A Crooked Creek Short Story

MK McClintock

Packsaddle Press

Montana

Packsaddle Press
Bigfork, Montana
Packsaddle Press is an imprint of Cambron Publishing Group LLC

Published in the United States of America

McClintock, MK
"Clara of Crooked Creek"; short story/MK McClintock
ISBN-10: 0-997089040
ISBN-13: 978-0997089042

Cover design by Potterton House Author Services
Field in Glacier National Park, Montana by fishysam | iStock
Gray Horse by Vicuschka | Dreamstime
Two Horses by Tainar | Dreamstime
Interior Image: Pine Cone by Cmwatercolors | Dreamstime

For my mother; a woman of uncommon courage and strength.

AUTHOR'S NOTE

A note on the Crooked Creek series . . .

Most of the stories in this series will be short stories or novelettes, but there will be at least two full-length novels, one of which will be a Christmas novel and another an exciting battle-and-romance-filled western adventure.

You'll have a chance to meet many characters from this unique Montana town, but for now, I hope you enjoy these glimpses into the people of Crooked Creek.

-MF

"Clara of Crooked Creek"

A short story

Crooked Creek, Montana Territory—May 1866

THE SILVER CREEK EXPRESS stagecoach rolled over rough roads against a backdrop of some of the most spectacular vistas Clara had ever seen. She was no stranger to lush meadows, but the green fields of Connecticut paled in comparison to the thousands of acres spread out on either side of the dusty road.

Her smile widened at the sight of a pair of eagles dancing overhead. Clara's hand pressed against her chest when a herd of horses basked in their freedom as they ran across the abundant fields.

"Mama, look!"

"I see them, Alice." She expertly reached for her daughter before she fell on the passenger opposite them. Clara peeked around Alice to see out the window on the opposite side. Antlered animals, too many to count, moved as one against a backdrop of snow-capped mountains.

"What are they?" Alice asked.

"I believe they're elk. Do you remember the photographs from the book we brought? Tonight we'll take a look."

Alice turned to the man across from him. "Do you know?"

The man's brow shot up in apparent amusement. "Your ma is correct. They're elk." He looked to Clara. "You've come a long way."

"It is that evident?" With a pleasant smile on her face, Clara smoothed the lines of her gray-and-white striped traveling dress. Gideon had told her it highlighted her smoky blue eyes, though in hindsight, it might be a bit too elegant for their destination. Then again, she had not risked everything and ventured out west to relinquish all holds on her cultured upbringing.

The gentleman's mouth quirked. "Are you headed to Salt Lake City or Denver? Maybe even San Francisco?"

"We're going to Montana."

The man's eyes traveled the length of her, and his face reddened beneath his gray whiskers. "I don't reckon Montana's a place for a lady like yourself. It's a mite different from what I reckon you're used to."

Clara only smiled again and gazed out the window. "I do believe it's the perfect place." She turned her attention back to the gentleman, an older man who reminded her of her father, tall, with a stately appearance and military bearing. His clothes, clean if not a little worn, betrayed him as a man of some means.

"Are you from around here, sir?"

"Jesse Pickett's the name, ma'am. From Missouri, but I've spent a few years in these parts with the army. Missed Montana something fierce when my enlistment ended a few months ago, so I'm going back."

Clara wondered what a man of his age was still doing in the army, unless he served as an officer. "The war has been over for a year, Mr. Pickett."

"Not the war with the Indians, ma'am, or with the vigilantes."

Clara glanced at her daughter, but Alice remained oblivious to the conversation as she continued to watch the passing landscape out the stage window. "Vigilantes?"

"Nothing to worry yourself over, ma'am." The man also glanced at the young girl and lowered his voice. "The army knows what they're doing."

Clara did not share the man's confidence in the army. Although freedoms had been won and a country remained intact, had they not just lost countless lives? To speak so casually of killing men sent a shudder through Clara's body. She had loved one of those lives taken much too early.

TWO STAGECOACH WAY STATIONS later, and after a night in a log-sided hotel in the growing town called Bozeman, the stage lumbered through a vast valley of spring meadows lush with grass and wildflowers. Alice slept as only a child did, tucked beneath the arm of her mother. Jesse Pickett remained their traveling companion, regaling them with tales of Montana.

"Crooked Creek is a right nice town. Not much too it yet, but I reckon it won't be long before the area changes even more." Jesse started in on another story of mining when the stagecoach picked up speed, jostling Alice awake.

"Mama?"

"It's all right, darling." She looked at their companion whose lips had thinned into a grim line. "It is all right, is it not, Mr. Pickett?"

"Can't rightly say, ma'am. Only two reasons I can think of for a stage driver to run the horses like this, and neither are good." He leaned his head out the window, and the shooting began. He pulled himself back inside. "You hold onto your girl. This is going to be—"

More shots, the sound of panicked horses, and the sudden feeling of weightlessness as Clara and her daughter tumbled forward.

"Mama!"

Clara's arms surrounded her daughter, protecting her as gravity pushed them from one end of the coach to the next. They collided with Mr. Pickett, but he did not cry out. A torrid pain shot through her spine and another through her leg, but still she did not let go. Alice's cries were muffled by her mother's embrace.

A resounding calm engulfed them as Clara pressed a kiss to the top of her daughter's head and allowed the darkness to carry her away.

"SHE'S COMING AROUND."

Aware of a minor discomfort in her side, Clara tried to ignore the pain and raise her head.

"You don't want to do that yet."

The voice was soft, feminine, and incredibly comforting. She was aware of another presence in the room, wearing the musk of horse and pine-scented air. Clara inhaled, her thoughts drifting back to the first time those same smells drifted into the stagecoach window.

"Ma'am? Can you hear me?"

The man had a voice, a pleasant one that reminded her of Gideon. Her Gideon and their . . . "Alice."

She heard her own voice, weak and foreign. "Alice?"

"She's just fine. You took good care of her." The woman's voice soon had a face to match. Copper-colored hair framed kind features and concerned eyes. "That's right. Come on back to us."

Clara's consciousness returned fully and with it a searing ache on the front of her head. "Where's Alice?"

"You daughter is fine. You both took quite a spill out there. She's resting now." The woman came into focus. "I'm Dr. Latimer—Emma. You're in Crooked Creek."

"Clara." She pressed a hand to her forehead. "Clara Stowe. I'd like to sit up."

"You can, now that you have your vision back. Gently now, there you go." Emma remained close, but it was the strong arms of a man who helped her up. "This is my husband, Casey Latimer. He and the sheriff found you two days ago."

They had been on the stagecoach, almost to their new home, when . . . the frightful details flitted in and out of her memory. "What happened out there?"

Casey moved to the foot of the bed where Clara could see him clearly. "What do you remember, Mrs. Stowe?"

Clara did not correct his misconception on her married status. "My daughter and I were in the stage, somewhere after Bozeman." She took a deep breath and strained her ribs in the process. "There was a man traveling with us, a Mr. Pickett. We heard gunfire—I think it was gunfire—and suddenly the . . . we were falling and it seemed as though we'd never stop."

She watched the doctor and her husband exchange a brief glance. "What did happen?"

Casey crossed his arms against his chest, his expression bleak. "The stagecoach was ambushed. After the drivers were killed, it appears the horses lost control and the coach detached."

"The coach toppled somehow, didn't it?"

Casey nodded. "There was a hill near the road. The

coach didn't roll far, but enough to cause some damage. You and your daughter are lucky, Mrs. Stowe. Very lucky."

"Please, it's Clara." Clara attempted to calm the pounding in her head. She looked to Emma. "You're certain Alice is all right?"

"I promise. A few bruises, but you protected her well."

"You said she's resting."

Emma held Clara's wrist and then pressed the end of a stethoscope to Clara's chest. After a few seconds, she nodded and stepped back. "She is now. You've been out for two days, but we've kept her occupied. She's been sleeping most of the time, which is what she needed. When she wakes again, I'll bring her in to see you."

"Can't I go to her now?"

Emma shook her head and with a firm, yet gentle touch, kept Clara from rising. "You weren't as lucky as your daughter. You'll be fine, but I need to monitor you for a few days. Nothing is broken, but you have a rather large and unsightly bruise on your back and another on your leg. Can you move your toes?"

Clara preferred not to consider what she'd do if she could not walk out of this room on her own two feet. She closed her eyes and moved her toes. "It hurts, but they work."

"The pain is most likely from the compression on your lower back. The pressure should ease in a few days, though I'm afraid the pain will linger."

Casey drew her attention. "Peyton—that's Sheriff Sawyer—will want to talk with you when you're feeling up to it."

Clara nodded and accepted a cup of cloudy liquid

Emma handed to her. With a hesitant glance at the doctor, she swallowed half and pushed the cup away.

"I need you to drink it all."

With a grimace, Clara swallowed the remaining liquid and handed Emma the empty cup.

"You'll feel drowsy soon. Your body needs rest in order to heal itself."

Clara nodded and then looked to Casey. "Do you know who did this?"

"Not for certain." Casey relaxed his arms and shared another look with his wife who nodded once. "There's been some trouble on the stage lines caused by a small group of riders. Before two of them were captured last month, they numbered six—four white men, an Indian, and we believe a woman."

Clara shuddered. "I didn't see any of the riders. Mr.—wait, you said my daughter and I were lucky. What about Mr. Pickett?"

"I'm afraid he didn't make it."

WHEN CLARA OPENED HER eyes again, night had overtaken the day. One of the windows in the room had been left open a crack to allow fresh air to circulate in the room. A gentle shift of the bed brought Clara's head around where she peered into a pair of light brown eyes. "Hello, my darling."

"I waited and waited. I was a good girl."

"Yes, you were a very good girl." Clara opened her arms and waited for Alice to snuggle against her side.

"Are you hurt?"

"I'm all better now that you're here."

Emma entered the room carrying a tray laden with food. "Good to see you awake, and you have your color back." She lowered the tray onto a table and walked to the bed. "And I see our other patient found you. Alice and I have become friends, haven't we, Alice?"

The little girl nodded and offered up a small smile. Emma held out her hand. "Your mother has a visitor. How would you like to help me downstairs while they talk?"

Alice look to her mother. "Can I?"

Surprised at Alice's ease in the company of a stranger, Clara nodded. "Of course you may. You listen to Dr. Latimer."

Alice giggled. "Her name is Emma, like my doll."

Clara returned the smile. "Yes, it is."

Alice slid off the bed and slipped her hand into Emma's. As they departed, a man entered, tall and rugged with blond hair mussed by his hand after he removed his hat. His striking blue eyes were made even more brilliant by skin darkened from the sun. "Mrs. Stowe."

"You must be Sheriff Sawyer."

Clara watched as the sheriff carried the tray from the table to the bed and helped her situate it on her lap.

"Call me Peyton. Most folks around here do."

"Then it's only fair for me to tell you that I am not Mrs. anyone. I'm simply Clara."

Peyton's quick nod indicated he understood, yet he passed no judgment. "I've spoken with your daughter. She's bright and eager to help."

Clara found she could still laugh. "Alice takes after her father in that way. You've come regarding the accident."

Peyton nodded. "Casey relayed what you already told him, and I'm afraid I don't have much more to tell you. I just wanted to be sure that you and your daughter are well."

"We have Dr. Latimer to thank for our good health, and I'm told you and her husband. How did you find us?"

When the stage didn't come through as scheduled, we rode out. Casey's what you might call an unofficial deputy when I need him."

Clara straightened the spoon on the tray but made no move to raise it or sample the fragrant soup. "Mr. Pickett—the gentleman in the coach with us—I'm told he died."

Peyton shook his head. "He was gone when we got there, except it's him I came to ask you about."

"Oh?"

"He told you his name was Jesse Pickett, correct?"

Clara grew curious at Peyton's tone. "He did. He also said he was coming here."

"Did he say what his business was here?"

"Mining, though I only half-listened. We traveled in the same direction for a few days." Clara straightened the best she could. "Did you know Mr. Pickett?"

"I did not, but there is a family not far from here by the name of Pickett, and I'd like to be sure of my information before notifying them."

"I'm sorry, but he didn't speak of family, only mining and soldiering."

"I appreciate your help." Peyton stepped closer to the bed. His eyes held concern and he glanced over his shoulder as though expecting someone to walk through. "Do you plan to stay in these parts?"

"I've bought a house here, and it's my plan to open an inn."

Peyton's eyes narrowed. "I heard tell of a man from

Connecticut purchased the big house that used to be owned by the miner, Mr. Cromwell."

"Yes, my father purchased it on my behalf, but I assure you I have the paperwork in order. I am the rightful owner."

Peyton held up his hands and smiled in a way that eased Clara's troubles. "I'm not questioning you, and it's not uncommon. I had thought at first it might be your husband."

Clara felt as though the words she wished to confess lodged in her throat, and she could do nothing to release them.

"It's no one's business. You'll find Crooked Creek is a good and understanding community with plenty of strong-minded women." He grinned. "It's takes gumption to come out here on your own. I imagine you'll do just fine."

TWO DAYS LATER, EMMA announced that Clara was fit to leave the clinic. Clara eased into the last of her clothing and faced the doctor. "I can't thank you enough for what you've done. Especially for taking such good care of Alice."

"Well, it's my job, and I can't take all the credit for Alice. Briley, that's Peyton's wife, has been teaching your daughter how to sew."

Clara was equally skeptical and surprised. "Alice, sewing? She's only five years old."

"A very bright five years."

Clara nodded. "She could read at age three, and loves to sketch, but she showed no interest in sewing when my grandmother tried to teach her." Of course, Clara thought, it wasn't the activity but rather the company. Although Clara knew how her grandmother felt about both Clara's life choices and having an illegitimate child, she had doted on Alice the way a grandmother should, and for that Clara was grateful. Still, her grandmother had been a strong member of the community, and society wasn't as forgiving. "I'd like to thank Briley for her kindness, though I'll admit nothing sounds better than home right now."

Emma walked with Clara down the stairs to the main room of the clinic. "I hope by home you mean Crooked Creek."

Clara stepped outside where Alice sat on a bench with another woman, presumably Briley. "I do hope so."

Alice saw her mother and slid off the bench to her feet. "Look what I did!" She held up a bit of what appeared to be a scrap of fabric. An uneven line of stitches ran across the length of the cloth.

"You've done a wonderful job, darling." Clara's eyes rose to meet the other woman's when she stood. "You must be Briley."

The woman's rich brown hair matched her eyes; her smile was warm and genuine. "Briley Sawyer."

Her musical voice surprised Clara. "You're Irish, as is my grandmother. She and my grandfather came over from Donegal."

"A truly lovely place. You'll find there are a few of us around these parts." Briley folded a square of white fabric and placed it in a basket on the bench. "My husband tells me you've purchased the Cromwell house."

Clara nodded. "I haven't seen it yet, but if it's as the banker described, then I intend to turn it into an inn."

Briley's brown eyes gleamed. "What a joy it would

be for this town. Though, I daresay we don't get too many visitors."

"I wouldn't suspect so, way out here." Clara indicated the basket. "May I look at what you just put away?"

Briley smiled when she handed Clara the handkerchief, though she was too quick to dismiss her own talents.

"This is fine work." Clara turned the cloth over in her hands. "The finest I've ever seen. My grandmother brought beautiful Irish lace back with her, but she couldn't manage stitching this delicate."

"Briley pulls a finer thread than anyone I've seen," Emma said.

Clara looked up from the fabric. "If you have more, I'd like to see it."

Surprised, Briley said, "The mercantile carries some of my work, and I've a few pieces at home."

"I would love to purchase some for the inn." Clara eased off the boardwalk as a wagon pulled around. She reached for her daughter's hand before she realized the driver was Casey Latimer.

Casey lifted Clara's bag into the back of the wagon while Emma kept a bracing arm around Clara's waist. "I'd rather you take it easy for a few more days. Casey will drive you home, and I'll check in on you this afternoon after I've seen to a few patients."

Casey lifted Alice first onto the seat of the buckboard. "You sit right there in the middle and you'll have the best view." Alice giggled and sat down with a little bounce. He helped Clara step onto the wheel and held her arm to steady her until she was seated.

Briley stepped up next to Emma and the wagon. "I'd like to come along with Emma this afternoon if you don't mind."

For the first time in five years, Clara meant it when she said, "I'd like that."

CASEY HELPED CLARA EASE down from the buckboard, and to Alice's delight, swung her through the air before lowering her to the ground.

"Can we do that again?"

He carried Clara's bag into the house and set it down in the foyer.

"We brought your trunks over—they'd been sitting at the sheriff's office while you were unconscious. I'm afraid two of them were damaged and everything rifled through. Did you have any valuables in those trunks?"

Clara shook her head and walked farther into the house, Alice's hand in hers. "Nothing that can't be replaced." Except Gideon's watch which she had carried on her person and had not thought of until now. She turned to Casey. "There was a silver watch pinned to my dress."

The look on his face told her what she suspected. "I'm sorry, but they took everything of value."

"Will the bad men find us here?"

Clara started to bend forward, the lingering pain in her side making it impossible to finish. Casey knelt on the wood floor in front of Alice.

"No one is going to hurt you or your ma again."

Alice swayed from side to side and considered. "Good. He smelled bad." She wrinkled her nose and with a small grin spun away from her mother.

"Alice, wait."

The girl stopped mid-skip and turned. "Yes, Mama?"

Clara's voice shook when she asked Alice to return to her side. Casey still knelt on the floor, his expression one of unease. "Alice, what do you mean the man smelled bad? Did you see him?"

Alice bobbed her head and then shrugged her small shoulders.

Casey gently laid his hands on those shoulders and repeated Clara's question. "Did you see the bad man, Alice?"

"Yes. He won't get us again, right?"

Casey exhaled on a slow, deep breath and smiled at the girl. "No, he won't."

When Casey rose, Clara's eyes met his. She wanted to ask him to send for the sheriff, to send for anyone who could keep her little girl safe. "Alice, why don't you explore the house a bit?" She quickly added, "Stay where I can hear you, darling."

When Alice skipped into the great room, Clara turned to Casey. "If this man knew Alice saw him, he probably wouldn't have left her alive."

"Not likely. I promise you'll be safe. I'll tell Peyton, but you don't need to worry. This is a quiet town—most of the time—and we look out for each other here."

Clara believed him, and she wasn't going to allow a single fear to turn her away from their new home. She did not fool herself into believing life on the frontier would be as easy as living on her parents' estate, but she didn't come west because it would be uncomplicated. She brought her daughter here to live a dream, and they would live it.

"The way I see it, we should have died when the stage rolled. I can't imagine coming that close to losing Alice again." Not after losing Gideon, she thought.

Casey nodded in understanding. "Alice will be safe, too. You have my word."

BY THE TIME CASEY had checked the house and made sure Clara's trunks and bags were within reach, which meant she wouldn't have to lift anything, the morning had turned into midday. Alice was napping on the settee in the parlor where Clara could keep an eye on her. She now stood in the foyer of the grand house, admiring the craftsmanship in the few pieces of furniture the previous owner had left behind.

She saw the cavernous space as it would be once she filled it with comfortable sofas and chairs, carefully selected end tables, beautiful lamps, and paintings throughout. Even the small details like Briley's beautiful, hand-sewn linens and the watercolor miniatures her parents collected from their travels, would help to make the inn feel more like a home.

Clara walked through the spacious great room, dining room, a kitchen large enough to cook a feast, a parlor, and what appeared to have been a study. A small room off the kitchen served as the laundry. She ventured up the wide staircase to the second level where four large bedrooms—all semi-furnished— offered varying views of the glorious landscape.

She made her way up the second staircase to the third floor where three bedrooms and a cozy sitting room filled the space. The furnishings had come with the price of the home, and though the previous owner had left behind only beds and a few pieces of furniture on the first and second floors, they would make do until what she ordered had arrived.

She ran her hand over the curve of a headboard and smiled. The memory of Gideon on their first night together before he left for the war floated to the surface.

They may not have all of the conveniences of home . . . no. Clara had to stop thinking of Connecticut as home. Their life was here now. Crooked Creek was home.

She returned to the main level and checked on her daughter who still slept. Alice would be hungry when she awoke. Clara was a fair cook when the occasion called for it, though she planned to hire someone far more skilled for the inn. A soft knock at the front door drew Clara out of the parlor and into the foyer where she welcomed Emma and Briley inside.

Briley kept watch over Alice while Emma examined Clara's wounds. "I had hoped to find you sleeping when I arrived. Casey told me what Alice said."

Clara fastened the front of her dress and moved to make tea. "I don't have much to offer you except tea, and I have a tin of biscuits we brought with us." Clara put the kettle on the stove, then turned back to Emma. "My arrival in Crooked Creek was planned meticulously, and I daresay, an ambush was not part of my plan." Clara glanced toward the kitchen door when she heard soft laughter and lowered her voice. "If anything had happened to Alice, I wouldn't forgive myself. She's all I have."

"I remember when I came out here with David, my first husband. He didn't want to stay, but I did. All manner of things went wrong our first few weeks here, but this place and these people are worth the effort." Emma sidled closer to Clara. "You won't leave, will you?"

Clara shook her head without a moment's thought. "I have no intention of running away when faced with a challenge, especially not on my first lucid day." They shared a laugh and quieted when Alice walked into the kitchen with Briley close behind.

"Mama, look!" Alice held out a delicate doll made of fabric scraps. It should have looked haphazard, but the deliberate blend of colors created a beautiful pattern. A small symbol was stitched on the dress, covering the doll's heart.

"It's lovely, darling." Clara looked at Briley. "You made this?"

Briley nodded. "I brought a few in this morning for the store."

Emma leaned in to look. "I haven't seen these before, Briley. What a fantastic idea. What is this over the heart?"

"'Tis a Claddagh. Friendship, love, and loyalty." Briley's eyes glistened with unshed tears. "My mum taught me when I was young."

"It's a precious gift." Clara handed the doll back to Alice. To Clara's surprise, Alice wrapped her arms around Briley and whispered, "Thank you."

THE WOMEN VISITED WHILE Alice's new doll made friends with the doll she'd brought from home. Emma excused herself. She had an appointment with a patient and once again asked Clara to rest, promising she would check on her tomorrow.

Briley remained, though she'd grown quiet watching Alice.

"Is something wrong?" Clara poured more tea into Briley's cup.

"No, sorry." Briley nodded toward the girl. "She reminds me of my sister. We lost her to a fever whilst still in Ireland."

"I'm so sorry." Clara's gaze drifted to her daughter.

Nothing more precious on the earth existed for Clara. "I can't imagine. I didn't have siblings."

Briley turned back to her new friend. "I had a brother. He was older, stronger, wiser, and I loved him dearly."

Clara didn't want to ask, but the same loss she experienced when Gideon died echoed in Briley's eyes. "The war?"

Briley nodded and wiped a tear from her cheek. "He and my father both. My father made it halfway through the war and died at Gettysburg. It wasn't his fight, or Michael's, but they believed in the cause."

"And Michael, your brother?"

Briley drew in a deep, shuddering breath. "He was killed at Appomattox. A friend who fought alongside him delivered the news himself when he returned to New York."

Clara reached across the table and covered Briley's hands with her own.

"I don't speak of it often," Briley confessed. "Peyton knows, of course. I have so few reminders of my life before coming here, but Alice . . . it's good to remember."

Clara squeezed Briley's hands, a gesture of comfort, though she wondered how anyone who had suffered such loss could find relief. No amount of good will had helped Clara overcome the sadness of losing Gideon. "I lost Alice's father to the war. He died at Leesburg." Clara looked over at her daughter who had fallen asleep on her blanket, holding both dolls. "Two months after Alice's birth. He never knew he was going to be a father."

Briley turned her hands and held Clara's. A special and unbreakable bond formed between the two women in that solemn moment.

"Did your family approve of you coming west?"

Clara leaned back then and laughed, though she heard the exhaustion in her own voice. "It wasn't about their approval. You see . . ." she glanced again at Alice and said quietly, "Gideon and I weren't married."

"I see."

Clara sensed Briley's gaze on her and looked back. "We had planned to marry, the war began, and Gideon wanted to serve. We were foolish enough not to question if he would return, but he gave me Alice before he left."

Briley did not look upon her as a woman bearing the mark of a sinner but rather as a new friend whose well of compassion would never run dry.

CLARA WOKE THE NEXT morning to a glimpse of sunlight as it filtered through the bedroom window. She'd left it open the night before with the curtains pulled back to allow fresh air to fill the room. Her family used to go on holiday once a summer to the ocean, and she loved the crash of waves against the rocks and beach. However, the invigorating salt-water air couldn't compare to the purity of what now filled her lungs. With the scent of pine on every breath, and the air crisp and pristine, she paused to inhale deeply.

She reached for her robe at the end of the bed and slipped into it as she ventured across the hall to her daughter's bedroom. Alice had been excited when she saw the large bed in what was to be her new room, though Clara would need to add some feminine touches for a young girl. With Alice still deep in sleep, Clara washed and dressed, then made her way down the stairs to the main level. She opened the back door off the kitchen, pressing a hand against her side when she extended too far. Wincing, she wondered how long the bruises would pain her, and at the same time, she counted her blessings . . . poor Mr. Pickett.

A dim light cast colors through the morning sky as the sun crested the mountain peaks. Alice would sleep for another hour yet, and she had work to do.

She made use of the lavatory—hadn't Alice been surprised when she realized they didn't have indoor plumbing in Crooked Creek—and washed up at the basin in the sink. She mentally planned out the four bedrooms she would use for guests, and a thrill of excitement coursed through her. They didn't need the funds a small inn would bring, but she was determined to be useful, to prove her ability to survive on her own and support a child. Her grandmother's hurtful words of doubt and how her granddaughter needed a husband echoed through her thoughts before Clara could stop them. Why would a woman with everything she could ever need or desire, want to trade in her privileged life for one in the wilderness? Clara quickly pushed the unwanted question aside because she already knew the answer. It's what she and Gideon would have done together.

Clara heard a knock at the front door. When she entered the foyer, the pounding ceased, followed by a low whimper, scratching, and a hoarse plea for help.

She opened the front door an inch to see outside. A dog thumped its shaggy tail against the wood, laid down, and whimpered. The animal wasn't alone on the veranda. "Good heavens."

THE YOUNG BOY'S WEIGHT, though slight, was more than Clara could handle on her own. She managed to help him into the parlor, where the only furnishings were a settee and end table. She eased him down, pausing when a soft moan escaped the boy's lips.

Clara spun around when she heard the patter of stockinged feet on the floor. "Alice, come here please."

The young girl hurried to her mother's side, her honey-colored hair half loose and half in a braid.

"Can you do something for me?"

The little girl nodded and then turned at the sound of another whimper. "Puppy!"

"Yes, a puppy. Now Alice, can you stay right here and keep the puppy and this boy company?"

The girl's eyes widened in question, though instead of voicing fear, she bobbed her head, lowered herself to the ground, and rested a hand on the dog's head. Clara spared a glance to the boy and rushed to the kitchen. She unearthed a bowl and pumped water, though precious little came out. She lifted the hem of her petticoat, slid it across the edge of the table until it tore, and rent the fabric to create two cloths.

Back in the parlor, Alice still sat on the floor, the dog's head resting in her lap. The boy's face appeared paler somehow, but Clara could not see any visible injuries. "You did well, Alice." Aware of her daughter's nearness, but unwilling to send her into another room at the moment, Clara dampened one of the makeshift cloths and smoothed it over the boy's head to wipe away the dirt. A few small scratches appeared.

"What's wrong?"

"I don't know, sweetheart." The boy needed a doctor, but Clara couldn't leave him alone or alone with Alice while she fetched Emma. She moved aside his clothing the best she could but saw no blood. "I need you to come with me please." With Alice's hand in her own, Clara moved them quickly to the front door that had remained open. "Alice, stay right here in the doorway where I may see you."

"Yes, Mama,"

Clara lifted her skirts and ran down the steps. A wider road leading into town crossed with the one to the house. She spotted a man riding away from town, but she had little choice. "Excuse me!"

The man turned and rode back to where she stood. He wore clothing similar to those of Casey and Peyton, except for the strange leather boots he wore that appeared to mold to his skin.

"Mrs. Stowe?" The man was without hat, but he nodded once. "Carson White Eagle, ma'am. Emma mentioned you to my wife." He looked behind her, no doubt seeing both the open door and Alice. "Is everything all right?"

"No. Please, Mr. White Eagle, I need some help."

Carson needed no other information. He dismounted, secured his horse, and followed Clara inside the house. She led him to the parlor where the boy had remained laid out on the settee, unconscious. "He was at my front door this morning. I don't see any injuries, but he needs a doctor. I had no way to take him. Is Emma in town?"

Carson nodded. "I just rode by there. She's been at the clinic all night with a patient. Casey and my wife are there with her, too." He knelt in front of the boy and with great care and efficiency, moved his hands up and down the boy's legs and over his arms. "I don't feel anything broken." Carson gently lifted the boy into his arms.

"Alice, stay here please and watch over the puppy, will you?"

Alice smiled in reply while Clara followed Carson outside and to his horse.

"Can you manage him for a minute?"

Uncertain, Clara nodded and allowed Carson to transfer the boy into her arms while he swung up into the saddle. He took the boy's weight from her. "Don't worry about the boy, Mrs. Stowe. Emma will take good care of him."

Clara watched as Carson rode away from the large house nestled in the pine trees, the boy safe in his arms.

ALICE DIDN'T UNDERSTAND WHAT had happened, only that a young boy not much older than herself was hurt and he had a puppy. She had refused to leave the dog's side, which made dressing her more difficult. The dog surprised Clara by remaining behind when Carson rode away with the boy. Once Alice was dressed, it was still early for breakfast. Clara hoped the small eatery she saw in town was open, but first, they'd check in at the clinic.

They walked to town with the puppy in tow. As much as Clara appreciated Emma and Casey leaving her a horse and wagon until she purchased her own, she would need lessons in both harnessing and driving. She continued to marvel at the vast differences between the East and the grand wilderness of the great West, which despite the influx of adventure seekers, miners, and cattlemen, managed to retain its glorious beauty.

A few heads turned as they passed storefronts and

a few wood-sided houses. Clara smoothed the front of her gray silk dress, though she knew it to be unwrinkled. The cool morning required little more than the square shawl for comfort. By a few of the thorough gazes sent her way, Clara suspected that the new wardrobe she had commissioned before her departure would be of little use to her in Montana. She knew the more convenient dresses with fastenings in the front would be necessary since she left her maid behind, but they were still the latest fashions. Ignoring the onlookers' questioning gazes, she smiled and continued to the clinic, all the while listening to Alice's excited questions about everything in sight.

"What's that?"

Clara stopped at the edge of the boardwalk in front of Emma's medical clinic. Her gaze followed her daughter's to an expansive meadow surrounded by thick trees, though Clara wasn't able to tell the difference between the various types of pines. Clara would be able to teach Alice everything she might have learned from a governess or tutors back in Connecticut, but her knowledge of their new surroundings was lacking.

She noticed only a small building, half erected, on the edge of town before the meadow opened up.

"It's the new schoolhouse, or it will be soon." A woman with light blond hair covered by a wide-brimmed hat sat atop a tall, gray horse. The woman dismounted and a pair of brilliant green eyes met Clara's. "Sorry if I startled you."

Clara returned the warm smile with one of her own. "You rode up without a sound."

"Lots of practice." The woman held out a gloved hand. "I'm Hattie White Eagle."

"I'm Clara Stowe, and this is my daughter, Alice." Clara accepted her hand and studied the woman. "I believe we've met your husband, Carson." Clara quickly went on to explain. "A young boy stumbled upon my doorstep early this morning and your husband was riding nearby. He brought the boy to Emma."

Hattie nodded toward the clinic. "In that case, I'll join you. You're already well-known in our little town."

Clara helped Alice skirt around a puddle of water in the road. "Is that so?"

"Not many people survive an accident like you did."

Clara preferred not to think about how close she and Alice had come to losing their lives. "We were lucky. Have you lived in Crooked Creek long?"

Hattie nodded. "My husband and I—my first husband—started a ranch a few months before the war broke out. No place else has ever felt like home, so I stayed."

Clara considered the confident woman beside her and wondered if she would be able to allow herself to love again. Perhaps she found it more difficult because Gideon had not been hers in every way. She had lost the man she loved and the father of her child, but she hadn't lost a husband.

"Are you all right?"

Clara turned to Hattie who watched her with curious eyes.

"Yes, just thinking how strong a woman must be to live out here on her own. I don't know how you or Emma managed for so long." Clara released a breath with soft laughter. "You don't know me, and I don't mean to speak of such personal matters."

A brief touch of Hattie's hand on her arm stopped

Clara, but it was Hattie's next words which brought her comfort. "You've come this far on your own, and anyone with the gumption to do that is stronger than they might think."

Clara watched Hattie secure her horse to the hitching post in front of Emma's clinic and step onto the boardwalk. "Why don't we see about the boy you found."

Alice turned to her mother. "Is he going to be all right?"

"I do hope so." Clara smiled at her daughter and stood next to Hattie who rang the silver bell hanging outside the clinic door. "We've brought his friend along to say hello." She indicated the dog who stood by Alice's side.

It was Carson who opened the door rather than Emma.

"Hattie, Mrs. Stowe."

Hattie's husband brushed a hand over his wife's arm in a simple and natural action that Clara envied. "Please, it's Clara. We've come to look in on the boy, if we may."

Carson nodded toward a closed door on the far wall. "Emma's with him upstairs now. She said he'll be fine. Exhaustion and hunger seemed to be the cause."

Hattie removed her hat and loose strands of wavy, blond hair fell to her shoulders. "I'd better see if Emma needs any help." She exchanged a brief look with her husband, one that spoke of an immediate understanding shared by those who knew each other well. "Clara, I hope we'll have more time to talk again soon." She leaned forward to meet Alice at eye level. "It was very nice to meet you, Alice. If it's all right with your mother, I'll teach you how to ride a horse someday. Would you like that?"

Alice giggled and nodded. Hattie rose, tweaked Alice's nose, and disappeared behind the door Carson indicated earlier.

Clara guided Alice to the narrow bench along the wall and cautioned her to remain seated. She turned back to Carson. "I want to thank you for your help this morning. Your timing was fortuitous."

When Carson smiled, it reached his brilliant blue eyes. With the exception of a healthy tan from the sun, his heritage appeared no different than hers.

"I'm just glad the boy's all right. Must have given your little one a fright."

Clara glanced at Alice. "She's stronger than she looks and more worried about the boy . . . I'm sorry, do you know his name?"

Carson shook his head. "He was still unconscious when Emma scooted me from the room and only came down once to fill me in on his condition. As far as I know, the boy hasn't spoken yet." Carson's eyes drifted back to Alice. "Have you had breakfast yet? You probably haven't had a chance to stock up on provisions."

"It's early yet for breakfast. We'll go after . . ." She glanced at Carson when he chuckled. "Have I said something wrong?"

"Not at all, just your mention of the early hour. Bess—she and her husband run the small café—are open before the sun. Most folks around here get an early start."

Heat creeped into Clara's face. "We're accustomed to a different way. That is, breakfast was set for a specific hour. I suppose it will take more than a change of wardrobe to fit in."

"Nothing wrong with the way you look." He glanced at the door when they heard movement on the other side, then continued when the door remained closed. "My wife tells me you're opening up a hotel in that big house. I figure this town could use with all the refinement it can get."

"Thank you, Mr. White Eagle."

"Just Carson." He pulled a small wooden horse from his pocket and handed it to Alice. "A 'welcome to Crooked Creek' gift."

Alice's eyes brightened. "For me?"

"Sure is."

"That's a beautiful horse, Alice. What do you say?"

"Thank you, Mr. White . . . uh."

Carson chuckled. "Carson's a mite easier."

Alice responded with a grin and turned her attention to the intricately carved wooden horse.

"That's very kind. Thank you."

Carson shrugged. "I like to keep my hands busy. Finished that one while I was waiting for news on the boy. Who's your friend?" He reached out and rubbed the dog's ears. For his part, the animal wagged his tail and pushed his head into Carson's hands.

"He was with the boy, though he hasn't left Alice's side since. I'm not sure Emma would approve of him being inside."

"She's a stickler for cleanliness, but I'm sure she'll make an exception this once." Carson gave the dog another pat and then rose.

The door to the stairway opened and Emma stepped through. Her crowded waiting room didn't appear to surprise her. "Clara, I'm glad you've come. You've brought company."

Clara laid a hand on Alice's shoulder. "The dog

belongs to the boy. I thought perhaps it might help to see him."

"His name is Mason, that much I managed to get out of him. Except, he did say the word 'bandit' twice. Perhaps that's his name."

The dog perked up and thumped his tail against the floor. Rather than admonish them for bringing the dog into her clinic, Emma patted the puppy's head with her free hand. "Mason's sleeping again, but I'm sure he'll be happy to see Bandit when he wakes." Emma carried a bowl of water to the back door and tossed the contents onto the spring grass. When she returned, she stumbled, the bowl falling from her hands. Carson caught her before she hit the floor. The bowl didn't fare too well. Alice's worried cry echoed Clara's silent one as she rushed to the doctor's side.

"How long has it been since you've slept, Emma?" Carson asked, his voice tight and filled with concern.

"I have two other patients upstairs who needed tending." She righted herself with Carson's help, but both he and Clara remained close. "I'm fine, I promise."

Clara looked around the tidy clinic and wondered how Emma managed on her own. "Do you have anyone to help?"

"A good nurse is difficult to find, let alone another doctor in these parts. I manage pretty well . . . most of the time. Hattie knows a little about tending cuts and wounds, and Casey saw enough during the war to help." She smiled and took in a restorative breath.

Carson didn't appear convinced of his friend's ability to manage on her own, but after assuring him again that she was fine, he relented and stepped away. "I better go and help Casey and Peyton search for the boy's family." Carson grabbed his hat and exited the clinic.

Emma sat beside the young girl and tapped the wooden horse. "Are you going to name her?"

Alice looked at the horse and then at Emma. "I have to think about it."

Emma bit the inside of her lip to keep from grinning at Alice's serious tone over the importance of the wooden horse's name. "A wise decision. Such a horse should have a special name." Emma patted her hand and rose to stand by Clara.

"You have a way with her, as do others in this town." Clara lowered her voice and kept a close watch on her daughter. Bandit stretched out on the floor beside Alice. "She's always been a vivacious child, curious about everything. Alice isn't old enough to understand why people weren't kind or why she could not play with other children her age."

Emma covered Clara's hand with her own. "Her father?"

"Gone before he knew, before we had a chance to marry." The words, quiet and reserved, were not easy for Clara to say.

"She's a happy and healthy child. You've done well, Clara, and don't worry what people here might think. I spent most of my life in the East and came from a family not unlike your own."

"You're saying people around here won't judge us?"

Emma didn't answer immediately, and when she did, Clara appreciated her honesty. "Some will. It's the way of things, and times haven't changed enough for an unmarried woman with a child to be free of ridicule, but you'll find that most people in our little town will care more about the person you are than some of the . . . choices you may have made."

Clara released a slow breath and cast a loving gaze upon her daughter. "I can't quite say why this soon, but I feel as though I've found a home here. A place where Alice and I can make a new life, build something that will stand for all time, a legacy."

Emma began folding bandages, listening to Alice's soft voice in the background as her doll and new horse talked with each other. "Do you plan to do it alone?"

"Didn't you?"

"For a time." She set aside the first pile and stared on the second. "I wasn't sure I'd marry again, or love again, but when Casey came along my heart didn't give me a choice."

"I loved Alice's father very much. I'm not ready to love another again, not yet."

"There's plenty of time." Emma placed the folded white bandages on a shelf and returned with a tin and a bottle of clear liquid. She dropped various silver instruments into the liquid. "I learned early on that if I keep all of my surgical equipment disinfected not only before a surgery, but ongoing, it prevents infection." Emma laid out a fresh white cloth and one by one removed the instruments. "I say there's time, but we both know that's not always true. Neither of us had enough to love our men, but when it comes to matters of the heart, we can't be timekeepers."

Clara nodded and glanced at her daughter who appeared to have ended the conversation between the doll and horse. "Gideon and I were childhood friends before we were suddenly something more. But for now, I cannot consider courting when I have a daughter to raise and the inn to open."

"I expect you'll do well on both counts."

"Yes, well, I'm afraid I'll be in need of a new

wardrobe and a lot of help."

Alice rose from the bench, the doll and horse tucked beneath one arm. "I'm hungry."

"We'll go to breakfast, and then perhaps some shopping at the general store."

Alice's head bobbed up and down in agreement.

Clara turned back to Emma who spoke first.

"I disagree about you requiring a new wardrobe. It's been a long time since I've worn the latest fashions; they aren't practical for what I do, but you'll be running this town's first hotel. You might need a few everyday dresses for the work, but I imagine your guests will appreciate a hostess in all her finery. I certainly would." Emma finished cleaning the instruments and tucked those away in a velvet-lined wood box. "As for the help, what do you need?"

"I need to hire a cook and servers when I open the rooms and dining room, but a cook now. Two women to help with the cleaning and laundry, and someone who can help with repairs around the place."

"Sounds as though you'll need more than just a few people. Are you ready for that?"

"I have . . ." Clara looked down at her daughter who seemed quite intent on the conversation. "My father was generous."

"The town could certainly use another good employer."

Clara interpreted Emma's brisk nod as approval for her plan. "Might I post an advertisement somewhere? I'd like to hire locally, if possible."

"There are plenty of good people who could use the work. Mrs. O'Reilly—she prefers to be called Maeve—at the general store will know who's been looking for work. She can also help you out with any new clothing you need."

"Thank you." On impulse Clara walked around the exam table and hugged Emma. "For everything."

THEY ENJOYED A HEARTY breakfast at Bess's café before making their way to the mercantile. Bess had even taken a plate of scraps outside for Bandit. The dog meandered along beside them but stopped at the threshold of the general store and sat. He seemed content to wait for them outside, though it took some gentle maneuvering to convince Alice.

Maeve O'Reilly was not what Clara had expected in a shopkeeper in Montana. In truth, she didn't know what to expect, but a woman close to her grandmother's age with a ramrod straight back and beautiful silver hair gathered atop her head was not it.

"Briley Sawyer is our seamstress in town. Not a lot of call for new dresses, but there isn't anyone with a finer hand at stitching." Maeve pushed her spectacles back in place when they fell too far down her nose.

"I've met Briley. I plan to buy some of her work for the inn and commission a few pieces. She does lovely work."

"None lovelier in all the territory." Maeve brought out a small pad of paper and a pencil. "I'll be sure to tell Briley you're looking for new dresses—five you say, how about that—and she'll come by for measurements and such."

"That would be fine, thank you." Clara watched Alice walk across the store to a short shelf of books. Her own library of volumes her father was shipping out wouldn't arrive for a few weeks. One of her and Alice's greatest joys was reading together before bed, but she'd only brought a few of Alice's favorites. "We'll be looking at your books, and I could do with some provisions." She reached into her pocket. "I've made a list."

Maeve studied the piece of paper with the neat lettering. "A few items we'll need to order from Denver, but we'll get you everything. I can fill this and my grandson can deliver everything when he returns."

"I would be grateful, thank you." Clara added a few bills to the counter.

"This is too much." Maeve scooted half of the bills back.

"Please, put it on account as a deposit toward the dresses."

"I like you, Mrs. Stowe." Maeve slipped the money into a box and closed the lid. "Now, let's have a look at the books."

Alice had already picked out two from the shelf when the women joined her.

"Those have some mighty big words for a little girl."

"Alice reads quite well, even on her own."

Maeve peered at the girl. "How old are you?"

Alice held up one hand. "Five years. Mama says I'll be six years soon."

"Five years and already reading these big books? I'm quite impressed."

Clara nodded, swelling with pride for her daughter. "She has a gift for it."

"She's a mite young to be going to school, but I expect she'll fit in well enough."

"You have a school?"

Maeve nodded and carried the books they'd picked out to the counter. "They're building a new one on the edge of town. We don't have a teacher yet, or many students, but the town is optimistic."

OPTIMISM WAS EXACTLY WHAT Clara needed. No matter the challenges she'd faced, she and Alice had found a new home, and she would make it work for them both. They'd stopped at the clinic after the general store, but young Mason was asleep again after consuming only a small bowl of broth. Emma concluded that it had been quite a while since the boy had a decent meal. Clara thanked God and her parents for not turning her out when she confessed what she and Gideon had done. Even though they'd been old enough to understand the potential consequences of their indiscretion, love prevailed. The romance of war turned out to be far less romantic than anyone ever anticipated.

It was two hours before they made their way back home. They left the store with three new books and a few sweets for Alice. Clara had posted her advertisement on the store's board since the town lacked a newspaper, and Maeve had promised to send any prospective employees to the house. She caught herself and smiled. No, the inn, she thought with determination. The top floor of the grand house would be their personal residence, and the rest would be an inn. Clara admitted that her skills did not extend to running a business, but she'd been taught how to run a household. The rest she would learn. Alice would have a home filled with people who wouldn't judge either of them.

Clara's parents had hosted dinners and entertained guests on numerous occasions, until their friends had learned the truth relating to Alice's illegitimacy. They had discovered that Gideon's mother, who had refused to accept Alice as her granddaughter, had made it known that in no uncertain terms did Clara and Gideon have a child. Her heart ached whenever she remembered the woman's cruelty. Gideon had been one of the kindest and most generous men she'd ever known. His father had attempted to soothe the discord and welcome Alice into their lives, but the damage had been done. Society was unforgiving.

Her own parents had accepted the situation, though not without disappointment. They knew Clara's heart and loved little Alice unconditionally. However, as long as Clara's grandmother scorned Alice's birth for the scandal it caused, Alice would never have the life she deserved. Until now.

ONCE CLARA HAD TUCKED Alice in for her nap, she made lists of what she would need for each room. Most of the furnishings and accessories would be ordered from the East or one of the larger cities in the Midwest. She would inquire about local craftsman to build tables and chairs for the dining room. She planned to offer her guests both comfort and elegance.

A knock at the front door reminded her to add a smaller bell to her list, one guests could ring upon their arrival. Casey stood on the other side of the door, dust-covered and grim. He removed his hat when she asked him to come inside.

"Certainly. May I get you some coffee?" Clara studied his bleak features.

"Thank you, but I won't be long. It seems you deserve to know what we discovered seeing as how you saved the boy's life."

Confused, Clara said, "Emma saved Mason's life, not me."

Casey nodded. "There was a small camp two miles south of here on the creek. Not much to it except a wagon and a few belongings. We found the boy's sister and mother, both half-starved and . . . tied up. It's a wonder the boy escaped and made it this far."

"Will his mother and sister live?"

"Emma's with them now. Beyond that, we don't know."

Clara's hands tightened into fists, though she didn't know why. She forced herself to relax. "I hope you've arrested someone."

"We have. The boy's father and an older brother. They looked healthy enough and well-fed, like they hadn't been to the camp in a while. They also had a few bags of gold on them." Casey rubbed the edge of his black hat. "It appears to be a portion of the gold from the stagecoach you rode in on."

"I wasn't aware the stage carried gold. Only a portion?"

Casey nodded. "This particular group of outlaws hasn't ventured this far north before and may have brought the boy and father in to help. Most of the gold is still missing."

Clara looked up toward the ceiling where Alice slept three floors up. "Alice said she saw one of the men from the accident."

"Don't worry yourself about that. We'll do our best to get them to talk. I'd as soon leave your daughter out of this, and she may not remember as much as she thinks. It's hard enough for an adult to remember much in the face of fear."

Clara relaxed. "She's bright, and I have no doubt she'd remember. However, I do appreciate you leaving her out of this. She's been through too much already."

"She seems to be happy and settling in. She's young yet and may not be ready for school, though that's a question for Miss Patterson, the town's teacher." Casey managed a small grin. "I suspect Alice will have no trouble catching up with kids much older."

Clara returned the smile. "No, she won't. Where might I find Miss Patterson?"

"At the old schoolhouse. A fire a few months back destroyed the classroom. We're building a new one in the meadow, but for now you can find her most days in the church. She's holding classes there for now."

"I appreciate your help and for letting me know about Mason's family."

"You're part of this town now, and we help our own." Casey replaced the hat on his thick brown hair and stepped outside.

She stopped him before he stepped off the porch. "Does this sort of excitement happen often around here?"

"It's as quiet of a town as you can find in the West."

Casey didn't give her a direct answer, but it seemed it was the only answer she was going to get.

He swung up on his horse and turned toward her. "And Clara?"

She faced him, waiting.

"Don't discount what you did for the boy. You continue to think quickly on your feet, and you'll make a fine Montanan."

SILENCE FILLED THE LARGE house like a heavy weight. Since their arrival, Clara had found comfort in the quiet and stillness. Tonight, with the moon's glow illuminating the room and the night air motionless, the silence became a deafening reminder of their isolation.

Clara calmed her fearful imaginings. She would grow accustomed to the peace of her new surroundings. She pushed the bedcovers away, slipped into her robe, and walked across the hall to where Alice slept. Her chest rose and fell with steady breaths. Her doll and the horse Carson had given to her were nestled on the pillow beside her. Bandit was curled up at the foot of the bed while his soft whimpers told Clara he was dreaming. She walked across her daughter's room to gaze out the window. The moon cast its light across the land, driving away shadows here and creating others there.

Chiding herself for the useless worry, she returned to her bedroom. She heard a low growl before a hand snaked around her waist and another covered her mouth. Menacing words followed foul breath as the man spoke against her ear.

"Where's the gold?"

She shook her head to indicate she didn't know. The man squeezed harder. Her only thought was for Alice. She shook her head again and tried to pull away from his grasp, to no avail. The growling increased, this time closer.

"I ain't asking you again, lady. I saw the lawman come here after he took the gold. You tell me, and I'll let you and the pretty little girl live."

Fear turned to fury when he threatened Alice. With all her strength, she pulled back his fingers until they bent into an unnatural position. He slapped her and she kicked, forcing him to the floor in agony. Bandit clamped onto the man's leg. It bought her enough time to race back to her daughter's room. Alice was on the verge of waking. Clara closed the door, sent up a prayer, and ran down the stairs. She heard the man following her and hoped he would continue to do so.

Dread returned when the stranger caught up with her and tripped her. She fell and slid across the foyer floor. Before she could regain her footing, he hauled her up against him.

"Your girl will live if you tell me where the lawman took our gold."

"I swear to you, I don't know." He pressed the knife against her side. "He said most of the gold wasn't there, and the other men from the robbery must have it."

Clara heard a whimper from upstairs followed by her name. She couldn't go to her daughter. Her only hope was to keep him away from Alice.

The man spewed a string of filth from his mouth and pushed her toward the front door. "Open it."

Clara did as told. She would go anywhere if it meant keeping him away from Alice. The moonlight had dimmed in the last few minutes, and the subtle shift in nature saved her life.

"Drop!"

She closed her eyes, loosened her body, and fell to the porch. One of them stepped on her leg before she managed to roll out of the way. The scuffle didn't last long. She heard a loud thud and felt the porch vibrate. A pair of strong arms lifted her to her feet.

"Did he hurt you?"

Clara looked up at Peyton. "No." She said it again with more conviction. "No, we're all right. Is he . . . dead?"

"Not yet." Clara spun around to see Casey hefting another man—this one much smaller—onto the back of his horse.

"You sure you're not hurt? Look at me, Clara."

She faced Peyton and tried to calm her accelerated heart. "I'm sure. They were after the gold."

Peyton picked up his hat and proceeded to tie the hands of the man he felled. "We caught another one trying to sneak into the clinic."

Suddenly mindful that she wore only her nightclothes, Clara secured the edges of her robe. "Were they the men from the camp?"

"No. We got the father to talk. He and his older son helped these men rob the stage you came in on. It seems the father and son took all of the gold. Carson is riding out to get it now." Peyton dragged the man to his feet, ignoring the moans. "I need you to go back inside now. You and Alice are safe."

"Peyton, wait. How did you know they'd be here?"

"We didn't. Their partner told us. He was young and scared and foolish enough to try and go after the family." Peyton handed his prisoner off to Casey and faced Clara. "You should know, it was the older son Alice saw the day of the accident. He saw her, too. No harm will come to her."

Clara didn't wait for the men to leave. She closed the door and rushed upstairs to find her daughter. Alice sat on the floor in the hall between their bedrooms, Bandit's head in her lap. A soft moan escaped the dog, and Clara knelt down beside them.

"Mama? What happened to Bandit?"

"It looks like he hurt his leg." Clara choked back her relief and pressed a kiss to Alice's cheek. "Why don't we make him comfortable, and tomorrow we'll see if Emma can fix him?"

"Can we sleep with you? We had a nightmare." Since her daughter still clutched her doll, she assumed the "we" also included the toy.

"Yes, for tonight. I think Bandit should stay with us, too." Clara gently lifted the dog into her arms and carried him into her room. She would worry about clean linens tomorrow. Bandit curled up at the foot of Clara's bed, and Alice climbed beneath the covers. Once the girl was settled, Bandit gingerly scooted toward her, resting his head on her covered legs.

CLARA AND ALICE RETURNED to the clinic the following morning after breakfast at Bess's café. She needed the comfort of people and noise. Alice had asked questions regarding the night before, believing what she heard had been a nightmare. However, her primary concern was for Bandit, who to Clara's surprise, had jumped from the bed without assistance. Still, she insisted Bandit see the doctor.

The door to Emma's clinic stood open. The doctor sat at her desk looking over a thick book.

"I hope we're not disturbing you."

Emma glanced up and then closed the text. "Of course not. I'm researching unusual symptoms a patient came in with earlier." She tweaked Alice's nose and lowered herself to the girl's level. "Mason, the boy you helped save, is getting better. He's awake now, and I'm sure he'd like some company. Do you and Bandit want to come upstairs?"

Alice tilted her head back. "May I?"

"You may. I think Mason would like a visit."

Alice turned back to Emma. "Can you fix Bandit's leg first?"

Emma knelt down next to Bandit. "How did he get hurt?"

Alice shrugged. "Mama said he was a really good

puppy, and he's happy now. He was sad before."

Emma glanced up at Clara. "I see." She ran her hands up and down the dog's legs. "It doesn't appear anything's broken. He might just have a little bruise."

"He'll get better." Alice's words conveyed an innocent confidence found only in the young.

"Yes, he will. I think Mason would like to see Bandit now." Emma reached for the girl's hand and said to Clara, "I'll be right back. Hattie is up there now with the boy—she's giving me a hand today. Alice will be looked after."

Clara nodded and watched Emma escort her daughter upstairs, smiling as she listened to Alice's cheerful chatter. Clara walked to the open door and looked out to the street. Spring had settled like a soft blanket of sunshine over the town.

"Your girl is a treasure."

Clara turned at the sound of Emma's voice. "Yes, she is, and she's taken with you. You'd make an amazing mother."

Emma's hand slid over the top of her flat belly. "I do hope you're right. Casey and I will want to borrow Alice for the practice."

Clara's eyes welled. "A baby." She remembered the fear, the excitement, the worry, and the joy she experienced the day she learned she'd become a mother. "Congratulations."

"Don't go crying or you'll get me started." Emma laughed and wiped a hand over her eyes. "I've decided I want a daughter just like your Alice. A little girl would be nice. Then again, I'd be happy with a boy who looked like his father."

"Then they'll be the best of friends, even with the years between them."

Emma stilled. "You're staying for good then. I worried you might have second thoughts after this mess, but Casey told me that New England women don't scare easily."

"He was speaking of you."

Emma nodded. "And of you and Dailey. Hattie's been here the longest, but she's not from these parts either. We've all been touched by tragedy and heartache, and we'll carry those memories for the rest of our lives, but it's our adversities which have brought us all here, made us stronger."

Clara tugged the edges of her floral shawl closer together. "I would give anything to have him back. Gideon would have been a wonderful father. Alice is so much like him— strong, beautiful, with a good heart."

Emma stepped toward her friend. "Alice is like you, Clara. You are all of those and more. You'll always have a part of her father, and you'll see him whenever you look at her. I remained in the cabin David and I shared together because it was all I had left of my life with him. When Casey stumbled through my door, I realized there was enough room in my heart for David's memories and my love for Casey."

Clara walked to the narrow bench and lowered herself onto it. "I'm not strong enough yet, but I will get there. I believe that now."

Emma sat down beside Clara and wrapped an arm around her shoulders. "You will be."

Clara didn't share Emma's optimism when it came to her own heart, except she had moved on—her journey to Crooked Creek, a new home, a business, and now new friends. She'd moved on more than she had realized. Clara faced her friend. "What's going to happen to Mason's mother and sister? I suspect his father and brother will go to jail."

Emma's sigh sounded like one of regret. "Casey told me not an hour before you arrived. Susan, Mason's mother, and Ellen, his sister, will be all right, and of course, they'll have Mason. There are no charges against any of them. They were the ones abused, though I'm not sure yet what will become of them."

"Where will the men go?"

"I don't know. The nearest army fort or prison I would imagine." Emma rose and walked to her desk. "It's unlikely they'll see their family again."

Clara's choices since she first asked her father to buy the stately house in Crooked Creek, Montana Territory, had been based on impulse and a desire for a new and exciting life. She saw no reason to stop following her instincts. "When they're well enough, I'd like to hire them."

Emma crossed the rooms, absently lifting a bottle of powder from a shelf. "Hire who?"

"Susan and Ellen." At Emma's quirked brow, Clara continued. "I'm hiring staff for the inn, and there's no reason why they can't hire on, if they choose. There will be plenty of work to go around. I'll pay a fair wage and the inn will be a place where they can be proud to work."

"Clara, you haven't even met them yet."

Motivated to take the next step, Clara rose from the bench and grinned. "Why don't we remedy that?"

SUSAN AND ELLEN REED would need weeks of nourishment and rest before they would be fit to help at the inn. Those weeks would give Clara the time she needed to hire the remaining staff and order the remaining furnishings and sundry items needed to properly run a refined hotel in the West.

Susan and Ellen both cried when she offered the jobs. Clara would need to find them a place to live in town, and their wages would see to it they could live in relative comfort. Their lives would be different from this moment forward, much like Clara's.

Alice and Mason bonded over a small wooden horse she gifted to her new friend and decided to share Bandit. When her daughter returned downstairs with Briley without the new favorite gift in her hands, Alice said someone else needed it more. It was something Gideon would have said.

Clara sat on her front porch with a cup of tea after tucking Alice into bed for the night. A gentle breeze blew the trees and brought with it a song of spring. The creek for which the town was named meandered behind the house, and in the quiet night, Clara could hear the water rushing over smooth rocks as the tall grass swayed with the light wind.

She wrote to her father that evening. She told him of their new home, which she decided to call the Stowe Family Inn, a sentiment she thought Gideon would have appreciated. Clara told him of the town and the people she had met thus far, and how Alice had already made new friends. She left out the tale of the survival after the stagecoach crashed and of the unexpected visit from the miscreants, of course. Above all, she thanked him for making their new life in the majestic and wild Montana possible.

When Alice had asked about her own father and why he couldn't be with them, Clara held her daughter close and told her of a brave young man who fought gallantly and gave his life for the people he loved most.

It was time for him to join the angels, remaining forever in their hearts. Alice had liked the idea of her father as an angel watching over them from high above.

Gideon filled Clara's thoughts with every beautiful memory she carried in her heart. She could hear him at times whispering words of love and dreams. He would not want her to remain alone—this she knew in her soul—but for now, he joined her as the quiet, moonlight evening enveloped her in peace.

The End

Thank you for reading "Clara of Crooked Creek"!

More stories are coming to the Crooked Creek series.

If you'd like to share your thoughts or comments with MK, feel free to email her at mk@mcclintockmt.com.

If you'd like to share your thoughts with others, consider leaving an online review.

Don't miss out on future books. Sign up for MK's periodic newsletter at www.mkmcclintock.com/newsletter.

Interested in reading more by MK McClintock? Try her Montana Gallagher novels—stories about family, hope, love, and justice in nineteenth-century Montana territory. Available in print, large print, audiobook, and e-book.

The Historical Western Romance Montana Gallagher series in order:
Gallagher's Pride
Gallagher's Hope
Gallagher's Choice
An Angel Called Gallagher

You may also try her British Agent Novels, stories of mystery, adventure, and romance set in the Victorian British Isles. Available in print, large print, and e-book.

The Historical Romantic Mystery British Agent novels in order:
Alaina Claiborne
Blackwood Crossing
Clayton's Honor

Also try *A Home for Christmas: Short Story Collection*. A collection of three historical western short stories to inspire love and warm the heart, no matter the season. Set in Montana, Colorado, and Wyoming.

THE AUTHOR

MK McClintock is the award-winning author of historical romance and westerns, including the popular "Montana Gallagher" series and "British Agent" novels. She spins tales of romance, adventure, and mystery set in the 1800s. With her heart deeply rooted in the past and her mind always on adventure, she lives and writes in Montana.

Learn more about MK by visiting her website: http://www.mkmcclintock.com.

Made in the USA
Las Vegas, NV
19 August 2021

28461169R10032